Family Storybook Library

Friendship
Takes You Places

Stories About Love and Friendship

BOOK SIX

Friendship
Takes You Places

Stories About Love and Friendship

Introduction

Friendship takes you to places you've never been before and exposes you to experiences you've never had. Friends brighten our days and widen our worlds with their cheer, support, and encouragement. Friends are reliable, trustworthy, and help us to do what is right even when we don't yet know what that is!

Friendship is a powerful tool in "3-2-1 Blastoff!," in which the toys realize that together they can accomplish something that they couldn't do alone. In "Baloo Lends a Paw," Baloo helps his beloved Mowgli escape the cunning tiger, Shere Khan, even while realizing that the Man-cub belongs not with him, but with other men.

3-2-1 Blastoff!

from *Toy Story*

⸻❊⸻

When you work together,
you can accomplish anything.

Buzz and Woody, two of Andy's toys, had been captured by his cruel neighbor, Sid. They were abandoned in Sid's room filled with mutant toys—scary-looking creatures made from different toy parts.

Luckily, Sid had left his bedroom door open.

"We're free!" Woody cried.

Woody and Buzz hurried out the door. In another room, Buzz saw a TV ad for Buzz Lightyear toys. Shocked, he tried to fly,

but crashed at the bottom of the stairs, and one of his arms snapped off.

Woody picked up Buzz's arm and dragged Buzz back to Sid's room. Suddenly the mutant toys grabbed Buzz's arm and surrounded him. Then they backed away.

"Hey, Buzz!" cried Woody. "They fixed your arm! Well, what do you know—these guys are on our side."

Just then Sid ran into the room. The boy dropped his toolbox on a crate, trapping Woody underneath.

"Now," Sid said, "what'll I blow up?" He spied Buzz and cried, "To infinity and beyond!" Quickly he strapped a rocket to the toy's back.

Then it began to rain, and Sid had
to wait another day.

That night, after Sid had fallen asleep,
Woody whispered to Buzz, "Hey! See if you
can get this toolbox off the crate, will ya?
Then I'll get that rocket thing off you."

"Who cares if I get blown up?" Buzz replied
sadly. "I'm just a toy."

"Whoa, hey!" said Woody. "There's a kid
next door who thinks you're the greatest.
And it's not because you're a space ranger,
it's because you're a toy. His toy."

Buzz stood up and pushed the toolbox
off the crate. Woody wriggled free. Then
they had a new problem. The sun was
rising.

Sid woke up, grabbed Buzz, and headed
downstairs. Woody begged the mutant toys

for help. "Please," said Woody. "He's my
friend."

Woody and the mutant toys hurried
outside. As Sid was about to light the rocket,
the mutant toys marched toward the boy.

"We don't like being blown up or smashed or ripped to shreds," Woody shouted. "So, from now on—play nice!"

Sid had never heard his toys talk. He screamed and tore off for the house.

By working together, the toys had escaped!

Baloo Lends a Paw

from *The Jungle Book*

⎯⎯◦⊷⊶◦⎯⎯

Everyone needs help sometimes,
and friends are eager to give it.

Baloo the bear loved Mowgli more than any other animal in the jungle. He taught Mowgli all about the bare necessities of life. Sometimes he even forgot that Mowgli was really a Man-cub, and not a bear at all. So when Bagheera, the panther, reminded Baloo that Mowgli's place was in the village with the other men, Baloo felt very sad.

But Baloo knew that Bagheera was right. The cunning tiger, Shere Khan, was just waiting for his chance to pounce on the boy.

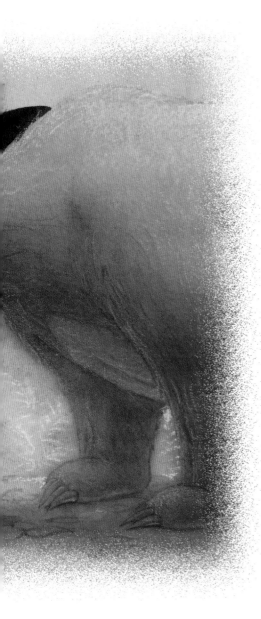

The sooner Mowgli was safely among his own kind, the better. But when Baloo tried to explain this to Mowgli, the boy got very angry.

"I'm not a man, I'm a bear, like you," he told Baloo.

Baloo scratched his head. He just wasn't very good at explaining things. "Now look, Mowgli. You've got to go back and that's all there is to it."

Mowgli stamped his foot. "I'm not going!" he shouted, and he dashed into the jungle.

Baloo ran after him, but the heavy bear was far too slow to catch up to the little boy. Mowgli was gone.

Mowgli roamed the jungle on his own. He didn't care what anyone said. The Man-cub was sure he could take care of himself just fine.

Suddenly a pair of hypnotic eyes entranced him. Kaa, the snake, had caught Mowgli in his coils! He was all set to make a meal out of the boy when a cold voice interrupted him.

"Give the mancub to me, Kaa!" snarled Shere Khan.

"Not so fast, Shere Khan!" shouted a familiar voice. It was Baloo!

"Get this kid out of here," Baloo ordered.
A group of vultures swooped down and
carried Mowgli to safety.

Mowgli watched as Baloo fought with

Shere Khan. Even the vultures were hoping Baloo would win. Baloo fought bravely for his little friend, but the tiger seemed to be winning.

A bolt of lightning struck a nearby tree. "Fire!" shouted the vultures. "Shere Khan is afraid of it!"

Mowgli quickly grabbed a burning branch and tied it to the tiger's tail. Shere Khan howled as the flames burned his fur, and raced away, never to be seen again.

Mowgli sighed in relief. He was safe, thanks to the vultures and his loyal friend, Baloo the bear.